MONA THE VAMPIRE

MONA THE VAMPIRE

Sonia Holleyman

Delacorte
Press

For Mum and Dad
and
Eva Louise Fowler

Published by Delacorte Press
Bantam Doubleday Dell Publishing Group, Inc.
666 Fifth Avenue, New York, New York 10103

First published in Great Britain in 1990 by Orchard Books.

Text and illustrations copyright ©Sonia Holleyman 1990

The trademark Delacorte Press ® is registered in the
U.S. Patent and Trademark Office.

Library of Congress Cataloging-in-Publication Data
Holleyman, Sonia.
    Mona the vampire/Sonia Holleyman.
        p.   cm.
        Summary: Mona disrupts her school and ballet
    classes when she pretends to be a vampire.
        ISBN 0−385−30286−X (tr.)—ISBN 0−385−30299−1
(lib. bdg.)
                    [1. Vampires—Fiction. 2.
Imagination—Fiction. 3. Behavior—Fiction.] I. Title.
    PZ7.HZ246Mo   1991
    [E]—dc20   90−3844
                                                         CIP
Manufactured in Belgium   AC

October 1991

10 9 8 7 6 5 4 3 2 1

It was a Friday evening. Mom had gone to karate class and Dad was reading Mona a terrific bedtime story. It was full of wicked witches and ghostly ghouls. It made her eyes pop and her blood curdle. Mona loved it. So did her cat, Fang.

"I'd like to be a vampire!" thought Mona
as she was brushing her teeth. "I could hang
upside down all night and never go to bed.
And Fang could scare all the teachers at
school...."

But Mona and Fang were soon fast asleep.

On Saturday morning Mona was up bright
and early. She had a busy day ahead. First
she needed a vampire cloak. The long
curtains in the dining room were just the
thing. Fang loved his new batwings.

Fang and Mona also played with Mom's makeup. Mona's plastic glow-in-the-dark fangs made her dribble a bit, but the overall effect was excellent.

"Behold Dracula's daughter!" she shrieked.

Mom made them a special monstrous
lunch. They had batwing soup, clammy
hammy sandwiches with tomato sauce,
and squashed fly pie. Fang's favorites were
the barbecued blood buns.

Fang was learning fast. Mona took him
to the backyard and taught him all the
important things vampires need to know, like
always wear clean undies. Then they played
hide-and-seek-a-vampire and suck-my-blood.

But even vampires are no match for a
karate expert like Mom, so when she said,
"I want your room as neat and tidy as a new
pin!" Mona did her best—with Fang's help.

On Monday morning Mona helped Mom by making her own sandwiches. She liked lots of tomato sauce: it was so finger-licking and fang-watering! She put her lunch box in her bag and stuffed Fang under her sweater. She was taking him to school.

Mona told her class all about vampires
and showed them some special vampire tricks.
No one would sit next to her anymore.

Mona always looked forward to gym and playing on the equipment. She practiced tying all her special knots. Fang loved it. He had so much to learn.

When Mona painted a picture on the classroom wall, the teacher shouted, "Enough is enough! I cannot have *that* child in my class!"

She sent for the principal. "Enough is enough!" shouted the principal. "Something must be done!"

So Mona went to join the ballet class, to calm her down. Fang went too.

Mona and Fang taught the good little
ballerinas some exciting new pointe work,
but Mr. Kersley, the teacher, didn't like it
one bit. He snapped, "Enough is enough!"
Luckily for him, it was time to go home.

"Hurray!" shouted Mona and Fang. They
didn't want to be calmed down.

Mona pedaled cheerfully home. Vampires didn't do ballet anyway. Her cape flapped gaily behind her as she sped along. It was a perfect day for vampiring.

The wind began to whistle and cold, dark rain began to fall. Mona decided to take a shortcut home, past the graveyard.

The storm grew worse. The lightning cast
eerie vampire shadows, the thunder roared
like a huge monster, and the wind shrieked
like a witch on a broomstick.

The shrieking and the clamoring woke up
the bats in the belfry. Mona pedaled faster.

Mona and Fang skidded around the corner and saw their house at the end of the block. It was a great relief. Even vampires get homesick.

And Mona was sick and tired. She stood miserably on the doormat and called for Mom. Fang sneezed.

"Enough is enough!" said Mom firmly, and made hot chocolate for them all. Then Mona was given a nice warm bath and put straight to bed.

Mona had disturbing dreams that night. Wicked witches and ghostly ghouls came around to play. They had heard all about Mona the Vampire!

In the morning a pale Mona washed off all her makeup and straightened up her room. She brushed the tangles out of her hair and put away her fangs. "I won't need these anymore!" she said. Fang agreed. No more catsup lunches and definitely no more bat-hanging from the ballet barre.

And that evening, when Mom was at karate, Dad read Mona a really terrific bedtime story....

But this time it was about space invaders.